W9-BGK-311

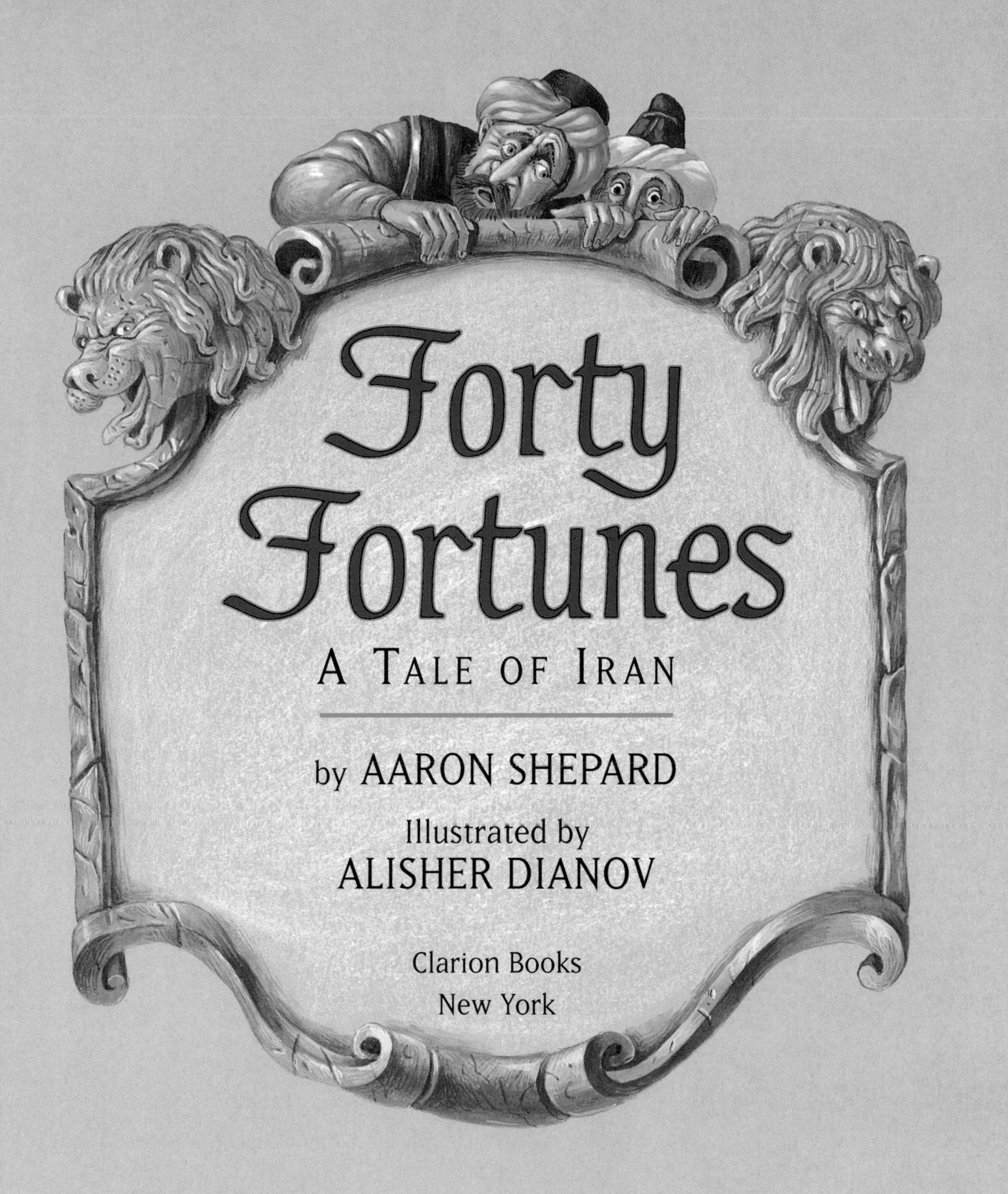

Forty Fortunes

A Tale of Iran

by AARON SHEPARD

Illustrated by
ALISHER DIANOV

Clarion Books
New York

For the people of Iran

—A.S.

For Olga Kondakova

—A.D.

Clarion Books
a Houghton Mifflin Company imprint
215 Park Avenue South
New York, NY 10003

Illustrations executed in watercolor
Text set in 16-point Matrix Book

Printed in Singapore

Library of Congress Cataloging-in-Publication Data
Shepard, Aaron.
Forty fortunes : a tale of Iran / retold by Aaron Shepard ; illustrated by Alisher Dianov.
p. cm.
Summary: A well-intentioned fortune-telling peasant unwittingly tricks a band of local thieves into returning the king's stolen treasure.
ISBN 0-395-81133-3
[1. Folklore—Iran. 2. Fairy tales. 3. Arabs—Folklore. 4. Folklore—Arab countries.]
I. Dianov, Alisher, ill. II. Title.
PZ8.S3425Fo 1999
398.2
[E]—DC21 97-19804
CIP
AC

TWP 10 9 8 7 6 5 4 3 2 1

How to say the names

Ahmed	AH-med
Iran	eer-ON
Isfahan	ISS-fah-hon
Jamell	juh-MEL

Once, in the royal city of Isfahan, there lived a young man named Ahmed, who had a wife named Jamell. He knew no special craft or trade, but he had a shovel and a pick, and as he told his wife, "If you can dig a hole, you can always earn enough to stay alive."

But that was not enough for Jamell.

One day, as she often did, Jamell went to the public bath to wash in the hot pool and chat with the other women. But at the entrance, the woman in charge told her, "You can't come in. The wife of the King's Royal Diviner is taking the whole place for herself."

"Who does she think she is?" protested Jamell. "Just because her husband tells fortunes!" But all she could do was return home, fuming all the way.

That evening, when Ahmed handed her his wages for the day, she said, "Look at these few measly coins! I won't put up with this any longer. Tomorrow you'll sit in the marketplace and be a diviner!"

"Jamell, are you insane?" said Ahmed. "What do I know about fortunetelling?"

"You don't need to know a thing," said Jamell. "When anyone brings you a question, you just throw the dice and mumble something that sounds wise. It's either that or I go home to the house of my father!"

So the next day, Ahmed sold his shovel and his pick and bought the dice and the board and the robe of a fortuneteller. Then he sat in the marketplace near the public bath.

Hardly had he gotten settled when there ran up to him the wife of one of the King's ministers.

"Diviner, you must help me! I wore my most precious ring to the bath today, and now it's missing. Please, tell me where it is!"

Ahmed gulped and cast the dice. As he desperately searched for something wise to say, he happened to glance up at the lady's sleeve. There he spied a small hole, and showing through the hole, a bit of her naked arm.

Of course, this was quite improper for a respectable lady, so Ahmed leaned forward and whispered urgently, "Madam, I see a hole."

"A what?" asked the lady, leaning closer.

"A hole! A hole!"

The lady brightened. "Of course! A hole!"

She rushed back to the bath and found the hole in the wall where she had hidden her ring for safekeeping. Then she came back out to Ahmed.

"God be praised!" she said. "You knew right where it was!" And to Ahmed's amazement, she gave him a gold coin.

That evening, when Jamell saw the coin and heard the story, she said, "You see? There's nothing to it!"

"God was merciful on this day," said Ahmed, "but I dare not test Him on another!"

"Nonsense," said Jamell. "If you want to keep your wife, you'll be back in the marketplace tomorrow."

Now, it happened that on that very night, at the palace of the King, the royal treasury was robbed. Forty pairs of hands carried away forty chests of gold and jewels.

The theft was reported next morning to the King. "Bring me my Royal Diviner and all his assistants," he commanded.

But though the fortunetellers cast their dice and mumbled quite wisely, not one could locate the thieves or the treasure.

"Frauds!" cried the King. "Throw them all in prison!"

Now, the King had heard about the fortuneteller who had found the ring of his minister's wife. So he sent two guards to the marketplace to bring Ahmed, who appeared trembling before him.

"Diviner," said the King, "my treasury has been robbed of forty chests. What can you tell me about the thieves?"

Ahmed thought quickly about forty chests being carried away. "Your Majesty, I can tell you there were . . . forty thieves."

"Amazing!" said the King. "None of my own diviners knew as much! But now you must find the thieves and the treasure."

Ahmed felt faint. "I'll . . . do my best, Your Majesty, but . . . but it will take some time."

"How long?" the King demanded.

"Uh . . . forty days, Your Majesty," said Ahmed, guessing the longest he could get. "One day for each thief."

"A long time indeed!" said the King. "Very well, you shall have it. If you succeed, I'll make you rich. If you don't, you'll rot with the others in prison!"

Back home, Ahmed told Jamell, "You see the trouble you have caused us? In forty days, the King will lock me away."

"Nonsense," said Jamell, "just find the chests. You found the ring, didn't you?"

"I tell you, Jamell, I found nothing! That was only by the grace of God. But this time there's no hope."

Ahmed took some dried dates, counted out forty, and placed them in a jar. "I will eat one of these dates each evening. That will tell me when my forty days are done."

Now, it happened that one of the King's own servants was one of the forty thieves, and he had heard the King speak with Ahmed. That same evening, he hurried to the thieves' meeting place and reported to their chief. "There is a diviner who says he will find the treasure and the thieves in forty days!"

"He's bluffing," said the chief. "But we can't afford to take chances. Change your clothes, then go to his house and find out what you can."

So the servant climbed up to the terrace on the flat roof of Ahmed's house, and he listened down the stairs that led inside. Just then, Ahmed took the first date from the jar and ate it. He told Jamell, "That's one."

The thief was so shaken, he nearly fell down the stairs. He hurried back to the meeting place and told the chief, "This diviner has amazing powers. Without seeing me, he knew I was on the roof! I clearly heard him say, 'That's one.'"

"You must have imagined it," said the chief. "Tomorrow night, two of you will go."

So the next night, the servant returned to Ahmed's roof with another of the thieves. As they were listening, Ahmed ate a second date and said, "That's two."

The thieves nearly tumbled over each other as they fled the roof and raced back to the chief. "He knew there were two of us!" said the servant. "We heard him say, 'That's two.'"

"It can't be!" said the chief.

So the night after that, he sent three of the thieves, and the next night four, then five, then six.

And so it went till the fortieth night, when the chief said, "This time, I'll go with you myself."

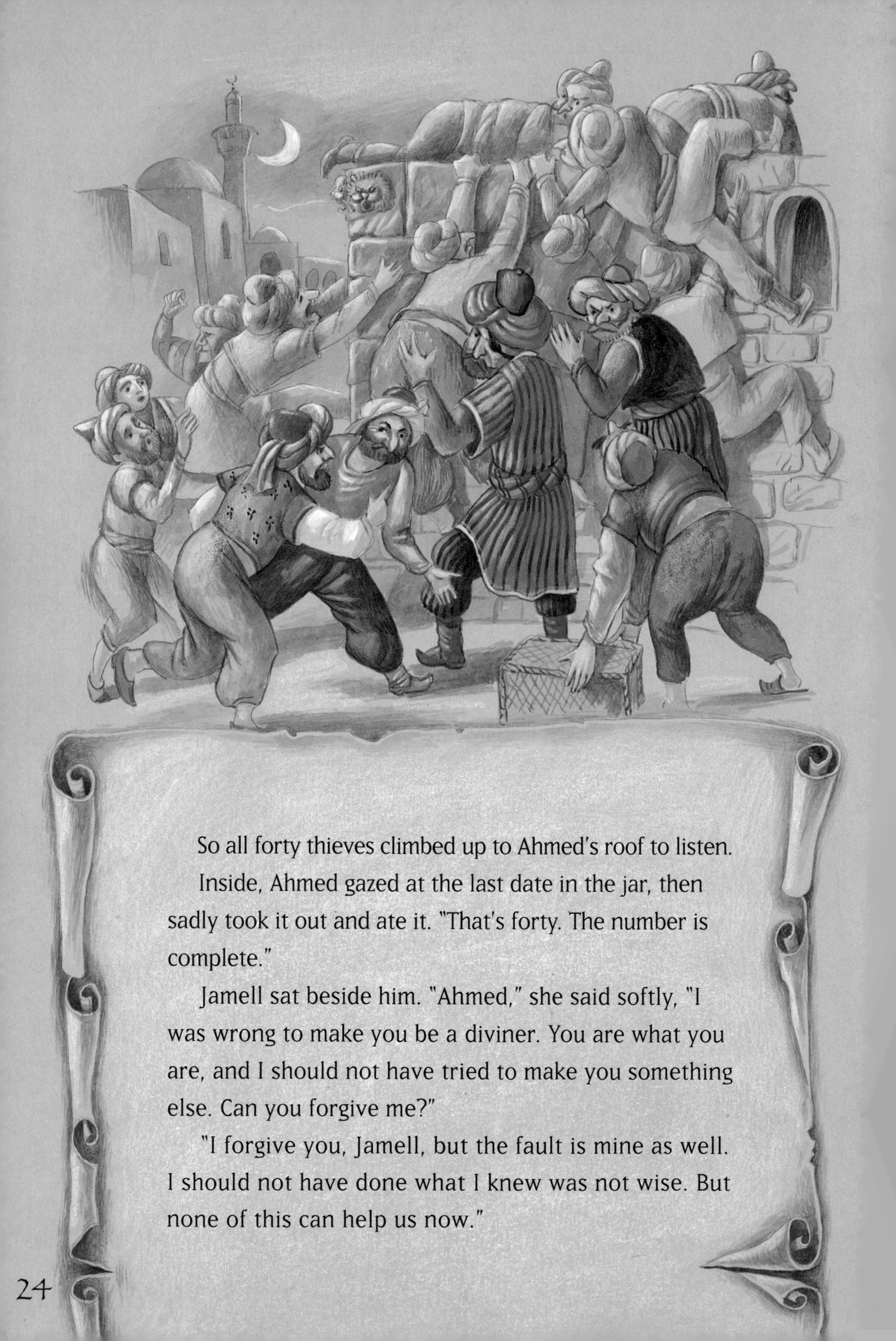

So all forty thieves climbed up to Ahmed's roof to listen.

Inside, Ahmed gazed at the last date in the jar, then sadly took it out and ate it. "That's forty. The number is complete."

Jamell sat beside him. "Ahmed," she said softly, "I was wrong to make you be a diviner. You are what you are, and I should not have tried to make you something else. Can you forgive me?"

"I forgive you, Jamell, but the fault is mine as well. I should not have done what I knew was not wise. But none of this can help us now."

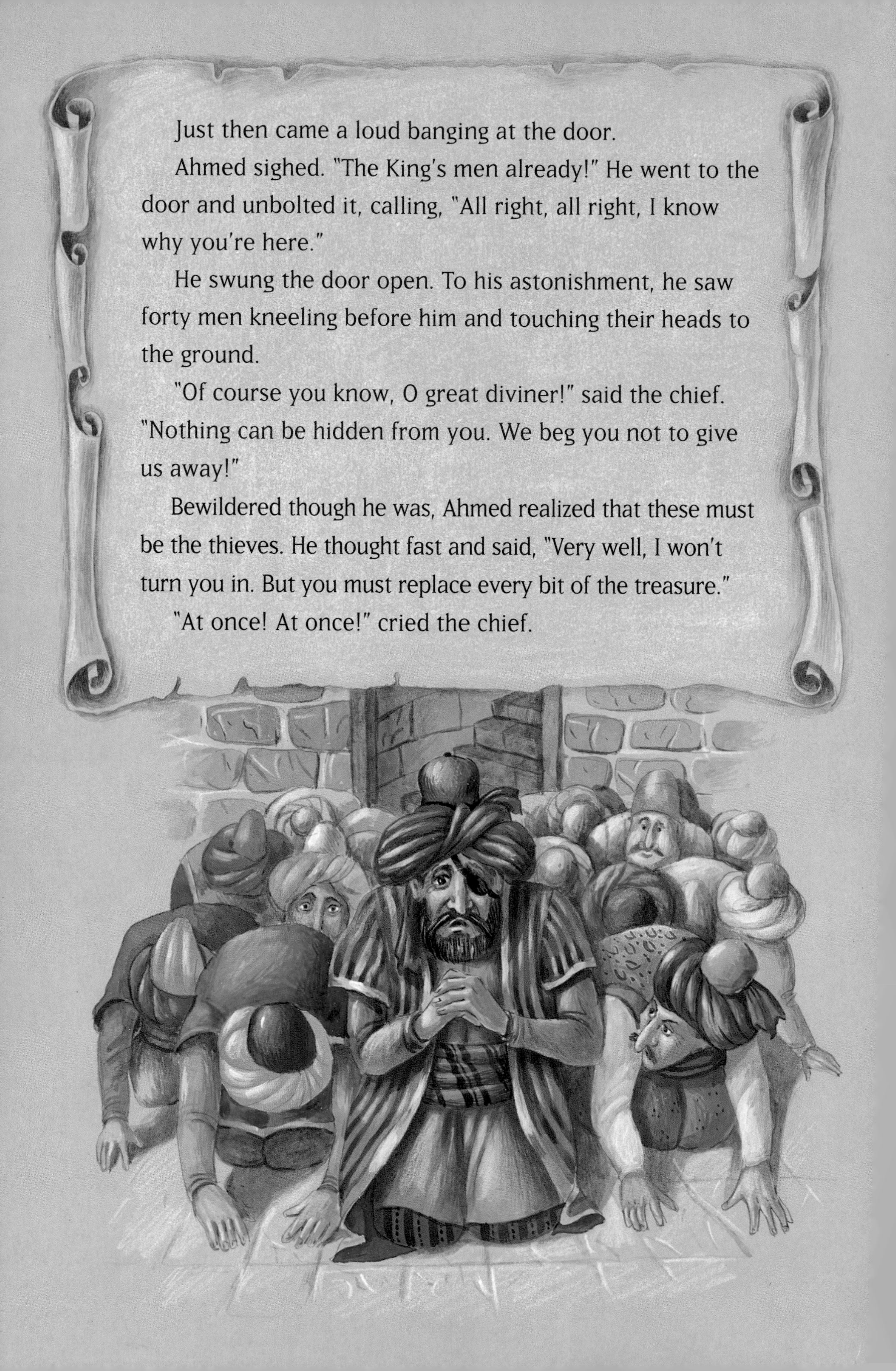

Just then came a loud banging at the door.

Ahmed sighed. "The King's men already!" He went to the door and unbolted it, calling, "All right, all right, I know why you're here."

He swung the door open. To his astonishment, he saw forty men kneeling before him and touching their heads to the ground.

"Of course you know, O great diviner!" said the chief. "Nothing can be hidden from you. We beg you not to give us away!"

Bewildered though he was, Ahmed realized that these must be the thieves. He thought fast and said, "Very well, I won't turn you in. But you must replace every bit of the treasure."

"At once! At once!" cried the chief.

And before the night was through, forty pairs of hands carried forty chests of gold and jewels back into the King's treasury.

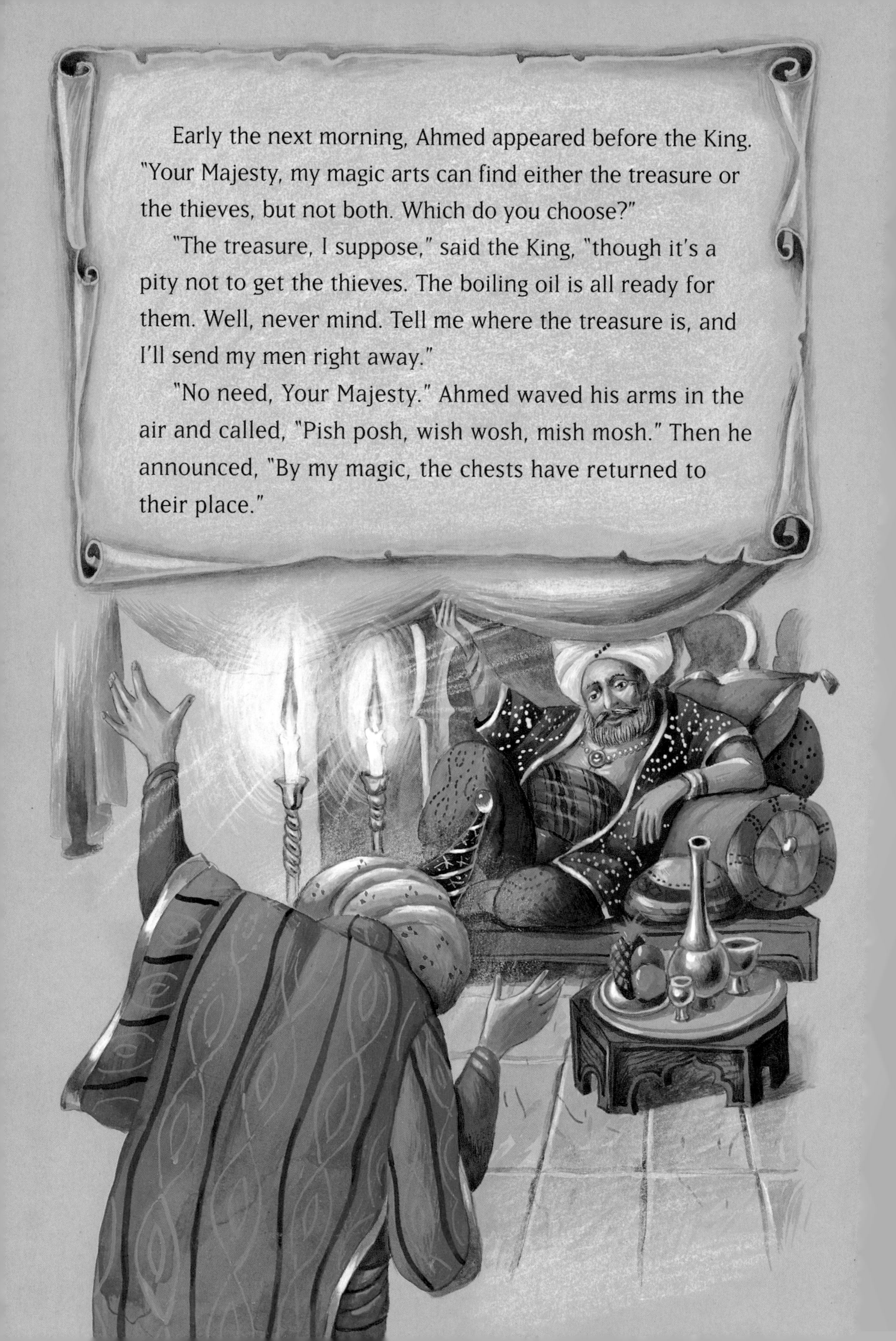

Early the next morning, Ahmed appeared before the King. "Your Majesty, my magic arts can find either the treasure or the thieves, but not both. Which do you choose?"

"The treasure, I suppose," said the King, "though it's a pity not to get the thieves. The boiling oil is all ready for them. Well, never mind. Tell me where the treasure is, and I'll send my men right away."

"No need, Your Majesty." Ahmed waved his arms in the air and called, "Pish posh, wish wosh, mish mosh." Then he announced, "By my magic, the chests have returned to their place."

The King himself went with Ahmed to the treasury and found it so. "You are truly the greatest fortuneteller of the age!" he declared. "From this day forth, you shall be my Royal Diviner!"

"Thank you, Your Majesty," said Ahmed with a bow, "but I'm afraid that's impossible. Finding and restoring your treasure was so difficult, it used up all my powers. I shall never be a diviner again."

"What a loss!" cried the King. "Then I must doubly reward you. Here, take two of these chests for your own."

So Ahmed returned home to Jamell, safe, rich, and a good deal wiser. And as any diviner could have foretold, they lived happily ever after.

ABOUT THE STORY

The story of the would-be fortuneteller is one of the most popular tales of Iran and the rest of the Islamic world, and is found in countless versions. You might enjoy looking for them in folktale collections and discovering his additional adventures.

Here are a few notes on elements of the story:

ISFAHAN. Isfahan was made the capital of Iran in 1598 by Shah Abbas the Great, and remained so for over a century. Under Abbas, the city became known as one of the most beautiful in the world, and it grew to be a major international center of commerce and the arts. This period is considered a Golden Age in Persian culture. (Persia is the former name of Iran.)

DIVINING/FORTUNETELLING. The attempt to discover hidden knowledge by mystic means seems to have been practiced in every culture throughout history. The Persian art of divining with dice is called raml (pronounced "RAH-mul"). The diviner throws a set of eight dice, then answers the question at hand by interpreting their pattern, often with the help of a book.

CLOTHES. Muslim law requires both women and men to dress "modestly" in public, keeping almost all of the body covered. The traditional covering for Iranian women is a garment called chador (pronounced "chah-DOR"). This is a one-piece cloak and shawl combined, most often black or dark blue, which wraps loosely around the woman's regular clothes. Though today the women of Iran are no longer forced to wear the chador, most of them do anyway.

PUBLIC BATHS. Trips to the public bath, or hammam, have been an important part of traditional social life in Iran and the Middle East. The bath is a building with large, shallow pools filled with hot water—an Eastern version of the hot tub. Both men and women use the bath, but in separate rooms or at separate times.

HOUSES. In Iran, the flat roofs of the traditional adobe houses are designed as living spaces. Here the family sleeps on summer nights to escape the heat indoors. Stairs lead to the roof from inside, and a high wall surrounds it for privacy.

Though many versions of this tale were consulted, I based my retelling chiefly on "The Story of the Fortune-Teller," in *Persian Tales,* collected and translated by D. L. R. and E. O. Lorimer (London: Macmillan, 1919). I am indebted also to the many students, teachers, and librarians who took part in my E-mail program, Works in Progress, during the first half of 1995. Their comments on an early draft were invaluable in guiding my revisions.

For a reader's theater script of this story, plus additional notes on divination and Iranian customs, visit my home page at www.aaronshep.com.

Aaron Shepard